Jasper and the Cheese

Written by Michèle Dufresne · Illustrated by Sterling Lamet

Pioneer Valley Educational Press, Inc.

Jasper was in the kitchen watching Mom.
Mom was making macaroni and cheese. Jasper **loved** macaroni and cheese.

"Oops!" said Mom.
A piece of cheese
rolled off the cutting board.
It went rolling across
the floor and under
the refrigerator.

Jasper ran after the cheese,
but it was too late!

Twitch, twitch
went Jasper's tail.
"Meow!" he cried. "Meow!"

"Oops!" said Mom.
Another piece of cheese
rolled off the cutting board.
It went rolling across
the floor and under
the stove.

Jasper ran after the cheese.

Twitch, twitch
went Jasper's tail.
"Meow!" cried Jasper. "Meow!"

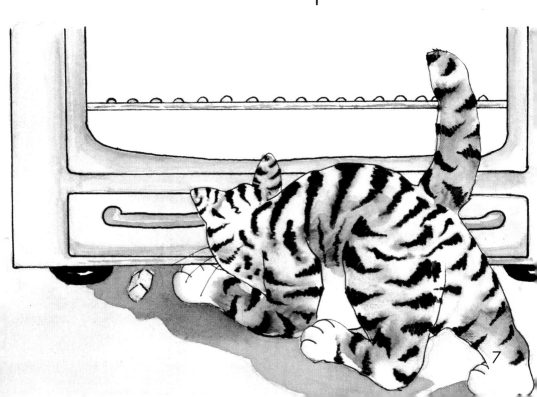

7

Jasper stuck his paw under the stove and tried to get the cheese.

Katie came into the kitchen.

"Meow!" cried Jasper.

"What's the matter, Jasper?" asked Katie.
She picked him up.

The mouse peeked out
from under
the refrigerator.

The mouse looked at Jasper.
Jasper looked at the mouse.
Twitch, twitch
went Jasper's tail.

Twitch, twitch
went the mouse's whiskers.

"Meow!" cried Jasper.
"**Meow**!"

Jasper the Cat

SET 2

Jasper and the Cheese
Jasper the Cat Set 2
Word Count: 159

PIONEER VALLEY **BOOKS**

pioneervalleybooks.com

ISBN 978-1-58453-397-9

9 781584 533979